For Sheila — thank you for giving this book life.

Text and illustrations copyright © 2019 by Scot Ritchie
Published in Canada and the USA in 2019 by Groundwood Books

Groundwood Books / House of Anansi Press
groundwoodbooks.com

We gratefully acknowledge for their financial support of our publishing program the
Canada Council for the Arts, the Ontario Arts Council and the Government of Canada.

Canada Council   Conseil des Arts
for the Arts   du Canada

ONTARIO ARTS COUNCIL
CONSEIL DES ARTS DE L'ONTARIO
an Ontario government agency
un organisme du gouvernement de l'Ontario

With the participation of the Government of Canada
Avec la participation du gouvernement du Canada | Canadä

Library and Archives Canada Cataloguing in Publication
Title: Owen at the park / [written and illustrated by] Scot Ritchie.
Names: Ritchie, Scot, author, illustrator.
Identifiers: Canadiana (print) 20189063041 | Canadiana (ebook) 2018906305X | ISBN 9781773061672
(hardcover) | ISBN 9781773061689 (EPUB) | ISBN 9781773062785 (Kindle)
Classification: LCC PS8635.I825 O94 2019 | DDC jC813/.6—dc23

The illustrations were first drawn in pencil, followed by fine line work in ink.
They were then scanned into the computer and colored in Photoshop.
Design by Michael Solomon
Printed and bound in Malaysia

MIX
Paper from
responsible sources
FSC   FSC® C012700
www.fsc.org

Owen
at the
Park

SCOT RITCHIE

GROUNDWOOD BOOKS
HOUSE OF ANANSI PRESS
Toronto   Berkeley

Owen worked in the park with his dad.

Most of the time, it was boring. Owen would sweep the long boulevard or rake leaves, while his dad mowed the lawn.

But once a week, there was a job
that Owen loved. And this morning,
he was going to do it by himself.

For a shy boy like Owen, the first part of the job was difficult.

"Just be friendly and firm," said his dad as he looked at his watch.

Owen stepped
onto the lawn.

He took a deep breath and walked up
to a family having a picnic. He delivered
his speech, but he mumbled, so he had
to say it again.

At first they looked confused, then
they gathered their things and hurried
away.

Some people had
to be woken up ...

or interrupted in the middle
of a game of checkers ...

or tapped on the shoulder
while reading a book.

One family didn't understand, so Owen had to act it out.

He tried to shoo some geese away, and they chased him all the way to the lake.

Owen had to hurry.
It was nearly time!

Owen ran through the park. Now he was shouting. He startled a baby, a sleeping dog, then a flock of starlings burst from the trees. It was so noisy, Owen covered his ears.

He reached the end of
the boulevard and looked
back. He had done it!

Owen couldn't stop smiling.
Now for the fun part.

Owen turned the tap.

Jets of water arched across the path, splashing tree trunks, flower beds and anybody who hadn't listened to Owen.

An hour later, the lawn
was soaked. Owen turned off
the tap.
Everything was quiet,
except for the water dripping
from the leaves.

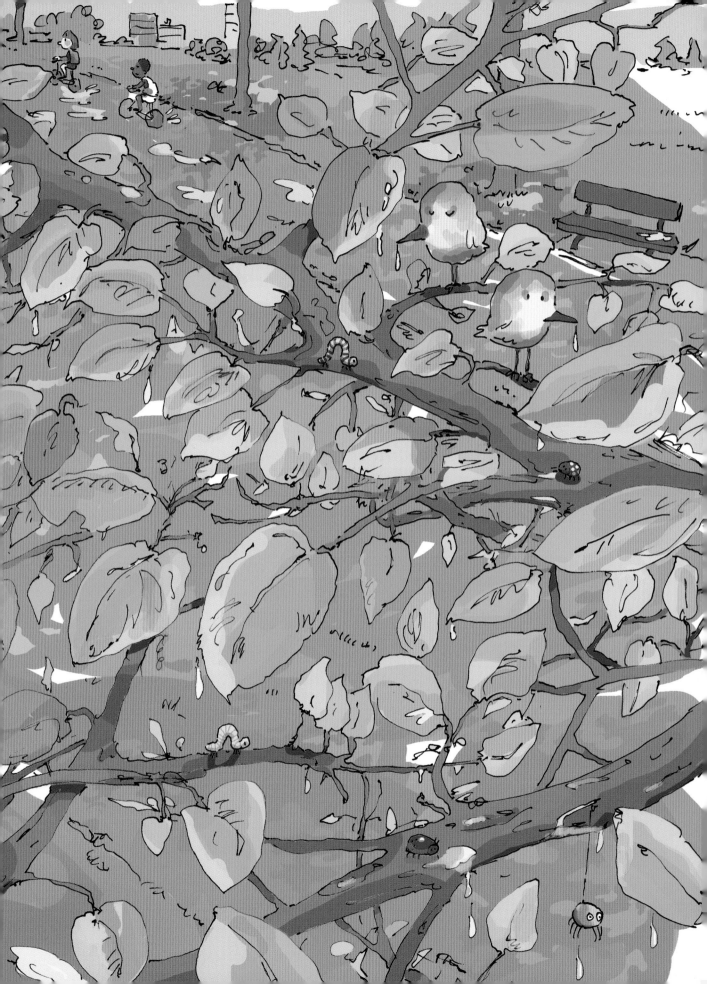

Author's Note

I was inspired to write this story after visiting Tiergarten, in Berlin, one of the most beautiful city parks in the world. Riding along the boulevard, I was taken by surprise when the sprinklers turned on. It was unexpected and fun, and the spray sent people running in all directions. I pedaled off the trail, dropped my bike and began taking pictures of the jets of water splashing onto tree trunks, the slow-moving visitors and the dry summer grass.

Later, as I rode away, I wondered about all the stories this park could tell.